fred
AGAIN

Also by Christine Nöstlinger:

Hello, Fred

Fred Again

Christine Nöstlinger

Translated by Anthea Bell

Illustrations by Erhard Dietl

SIMON & SCHUSTER
YOUNG BOOKS

Set in Palatino by Goodfellow & Egan Ltd, Cambridge
Printed and bound in Great Britain at The Guernsey Press

Simon & Schuster Young Books
Campus 400
Maylands Avenue
Hemel Hempstead HP2 7EZ

BRITISH LIBRARY CATALOGUING IN PUBLICATION DATA
available.

ISBN 0 7500 1181 5
ISBN 0 7500 1182 3 (Pbk)

CONTENTS

1. Fred Learns to Read

Fred is six years and six months old. He's rather small for his age. He has eyes as blue as cornflowers, and a cherry-red mouth. And he has plump pink cheeks, and no hair at all on his head. But Fred is not bald. He just gets his Dad to shave his head twice a week.

Before Fred had his head shaved, a lot of people thought he was a little girl. A little girl with curly blond hair. It upset Fred a lot.

Not that Fred doesn't like girls. He likes Gina, who lives next door, very much. In

fact he likes her better than any of the boys he knows.

Fred's Mum is sad about Fred's curly hair. She keeps saying, "You looked much nicer with your curls, Fred!"

But Fred would rather look not so nice, and more like a boy. Gina can't understand how he feels.

"Who cares if the greengrocer thinks you're my sister?" she says.

"I care!" says Fred. "It makes me

furious!"

"Well, I wouldn't mind at all if the greengrocer thought I was your brother," says Gina. "It would be really rather funny!"

"That would be different," says Fred.

"How come?" asks Gina.

Fred does not answer this question. Because he thinks it's better to be a boy. So a girl should feel glad if people mistake her for a boy. But it's an insult to a boy to be mistaken for a girl.

However, Gina wouldn't see that. She would tap her forehead and say, "You're daft!" And then Fred would say, "Daft yourself!" and Gina would thump him. So Fred would have to kick her. And then they would have a real quarrel, which wouldn't be a good thing.

Fred and Gina quarrel once a week anyway. And even the best friendship, thinks Fred, wouldn't stand up to two quarrels a week. You have to go easy on quarrelling.

One day in summer Gina and Fred went to the park. The little park opposite the block of flats where they live. They were on their way to the park playground. They wanted to go on the swings and the climbing frame.

But the seats of the swings had been

taken away, and the entire climbing frame was gone. There was a white notice with black letters, up on the fence of the ball-games area.

"There are three *a*s in those words," said Fred.

"And seven *e*s," said Gina.

"And the first letter of the first word is an *R*," said Fred.

"And the first letter of the next word is a *G*," said Gina. "If only it were Christmas," she added, "we'd be able to read what it says!" And she counted on her fingers. "September, October, November, December!" She nodded. "I bet we know how to read after six months at big school."

Then Gina went over to the sandbox. Fred didn't follow her. He went across to a big boy leaning on the fence beside the notice. "Please," he asked, "what does it

12

say on that notice?"

The big boy read the notice out. "Rides gone for repainting. Apologies for any inconvenience."

"Thanks," said Fred. He went over to the sandbox, whistling, his hands in his pockets, and sat down on the edge of it.

"You know something, Gina?" he said. "I can read already."

"You can't," said Gina.

"I can," said Fred. "That notice says the rides have gone for repainting, and ap – apologies for any incon – inconvenience."

"You didn't read it, you just asked the big boy," said Gina.

"That's not true! I *can* read!" shouted Fred.

"You're a stupid, beastly liar," shouted Gina.

Fred was going to say something nasty back, but he realized his voice was about to go squeaky any moment.

It was something that was always happening to Fred. Whenever he got upset his voice went all high and squeaky. And there was nothing he could do about it – except wait until he stopped feeling upset.

So Fred turned his back on Gina and looked at the ball-games area.

The big boy was still leaning on the fence. Another boy had joined him. This other boy had a football under his arm. A real leather football.

"If I were a bit bigger," thought Fred, "I could ask those two boys

14

to play football – just the three of us! And then we'd have a great match. And then we'd buy an ice cream at the ice cream van! And then we'd be friends! And Gina would realize she can't just call me a stupid liar and get away with it!"

Then Fred wondered if he might be big enough for the two boys already. He wasn't all that much shorter than they were. And some big boys are very nice and don't mind playing with smaller ones. Fred was just going to get up and go over to the two boys when Gina put her hand on his shoulder.

"Here, show-off!" she said, shoving a piece of paper under his nose. A crumpled, dirty piece of paper. Where the paper was not dirty it was pink, with black letters on it.

"Go on, then, read what it says," demanded Gina. There was a big girl

standing beside her. Gina pointed to the big girl. "She can read ever so well! She's going into the third class in September!"

"I don't feel like reading just now," squeaked Fred.

Gina laughed. The big girl laughed too. In a very nasty way. So Fred jumped up and put his tongue out at them both. "Yaaah!" he went, and then he ran home.

There was nobody at home but Lily. Fred's Dad was at work. So was his mum. And Fred's big brother Joe had gone round to see his friend Ollie.

Lily was a student. Fred's Mum paid her to come and look after Fred every summer, because nursery school was closed in summer, and Fred couldn't stay at home on his own. And Joe didn't like having to look after Fred.

"Lily, Lily!" squeaked Fred, when Lily opened the front door. "You must learn me to read, quick!"

"*Teach* you, you mean," said Lily. "I do the teaching; you do the learning!"

"Whatever you say," squeaked Fred. He went into his room and came back with a pile of picture books. He took the books into the kitchen and put them down on the kitchen table.

"I need to know how to read by lunchtime!" he squeaked.

"Can't be done, Tiddler," said Lily. (Lily always called Fred "Tiddler", but Fred didn't mind, because she often

called Joe "Tiddler", too, and Joe was not a bit small for his age.)

"Well then, by this evening," squeaked Fred.

"That can't be done either, Tiddler," said Lily. And she added, "Anyway, I haven't the faintest idea how to teach you to read. I'm not a teacher, am I?"

Fred could see that. At first he felt rather sad. But then he had a good idea.

Such a good idea that his voice went normal and deep and perfectly all right again. Fred got the book about the farmyard out of his pile of picture books. There was a picture on every page of the book, with two lines of words underneath. The first picture showed a fat pig. The words said:

"Piggy's fat and pink and pale,
Piggy has a curly tail."

Piggy's fat and pink and pale,
Piggy has a curly tail.

Mum had read Fred the picture book

over and over again and he knew the words off by heart.

The second picture showed a cow. The words said:

"Molly Moo is soft as silk.

She gives us butter, cream and milk."

Fred knew those words off by heart as well.

He looked through the farmyard picture book from the first page to the very last. He kept nodding as he looked at the pictures. Then he handed Lily the book and said, "Okay, ask me!" (When Joe took Mum a list of things he had to learn by heart for homework, and wanted her to test him, he always said, "Okay, ask me!")

And then Fred recited the words in the picture book, verse by verse. From the first page to the very last.

"Word-perfect, Tiddler," said Lily.

"But that's not good enough," said
Fred.

"Not good enough for what?" asked
Lily.

"It's a secret," said Fred.

Lily sat at the kitchen table slicing
carrots. The carrots were going to be part
of Fred's lunch.

Fred picked another book out of the
pile and pushed it over to Lily.

"Read me that book a hundred times,

please," he said.

"Don't be daft," said Lily.

"Well, maybe twenty times will do," said Fred.

"Three times is too many," said Lily.

Fred explained. He told Lily he had to learn the picture book off by heart, so hearing it read aloud just once wouldn't be enough.

Lily saw his point. She found Joe's tape recorder, put an empty cassette in it, and read the picture book aloud into the microphone. Then she showed Fred how to work the Play button and the Rewind button.

So Fred pressed Play and listened, muttering along with the tape, pressed Rewind and waited, pressed Play and listened, muttering along with the tape, pressed Rewind and waited and pressed Play and listened, muttering along with

the tape . . . until Lily said, "Tiddler, I can't stand any more of this! It's making my brain go soft!"

So Fred took the tape recorder into his room.

At teatime he asked Lily to listen to him.

"Word-perfect again, Tiddler," Lily said.

So then Fred got her to record a third picture book on tape.

And he went back to his room.

When Mum and Dad came home from work, and Joe got back from Ollie's, Fred was still in his room. A notice saying PLEASE DO NOT disturb hung on the door.

"He's learning his picture books by heart," said Lily.

"What for?" asked Mum and Dad. (Joe wasn't interested. He was never interested in knowing why Fred did something.)

"It's a secret," said Lily.

At suppertime Fred came out of his room with the three picture books under his arm.

This time Mum had to listen to him, because Lily had gone home.

Fred knew all the words of his three picture books. The words of the farmyard picture book, the words of the *Ten Little Indians* picture book, and the words of the

Mouse Birthday Party picture book.

"Well done, Fred dear," said Mum.

"Now I'm going over to Gina's," said Fred.

"Not tonight," said Dad. "After supper is too late to visit people."

"But I have to," said Fred.

"You don't have to," said Dad.

"Yes, I do," said Fred. "I'll have forgotten those blasted words again by tomorrow morning!"

"Fred!" cried Dad. "What language! You should be ashamed of yourself."

"He picks it up from you," said Mum.

"He didn't pick that up from me," said Dad.

"Yes, he did," said Joe. "When you

were looking for the car key yesterday, you said, 'Where's that blasted key?' You said it three times!"

"He's quite right!" said Mum.

"You keep out of this!" Dad shouted at Joe.

"I can say what I think, can't I?" said Joe.

"Of course you can!" said Mum.

Fred got down from his chair, picked up his three picture books and left the living room. As he opened the front door, Dad was yelling, "Well, even if a word of that kind does **happen** to slip out, that's no reason to repeat it!"

And as Fred quietly closed the front door, Mum was shouting, "Oh, I see! So you're an exception! You ought to be setting an example!"

It's the heatwave, thought Fred. They always quarrel at suppertime when it's hot like this.

Fred rang Gina's front door bell. Gina's Mum opened the door.

"It's something important," said Fred. "That's why I'm visiting so late!"

"Gina's in the bath," said Gina's Mum.

Fred went into the bathroom. There was a great mound of foam in the bathtub. Gina's head was sticking out of the foam.

"Okay, so you didn't believe me," said

Fred. He sat down on the linen basket and opened the farmyard book. "Well, I'm going to read aloud to you!"

"Mum, come here!" called Gina. "Fred's telling terrible lies again!"

Gina's Mum came into the bathroom. "I think you two had better settle this on your own," she said.

"No!" said Gina. "*I* can't read. You'll have to check that he doesn't cheat!"

So Gina's Mum stood behind Fred, and Fred started to read. He was rather crafty about it. He didn't just recite the words straight off. He pretended it was difficult reading them. "P- . . .Piggy's f-f-fat," he read. And, "M-Molly Moo is . . . is s-s-soft as – as silk!"

When Fred closed the third picture book, Gina's Mum said, 'He wasn't telling lies. He really can read!"

"So there!" said Fred. He put the

picture books under his arm and slid off the linen basket.

The mound of foam in the tub was much smaller now. Gina was sticking out of the foam down to her tummy button. "Are you cross with me?" she asked. "For not believing you?"

"Not a bit," said Fred generously. "Well, I must go home now."

"See you tomorrow, Freddie," Gina called after him.

Since then Gina has been getting Fred to read her all sorts of things. Street names, notices in the park, picture books, advertisements, the wording on boxes and cans. Even the notices on the board in the hall downstairs. And newspaper headlines too.

Fred enjoys it, and it's not very difficult, either, so long as there's no

one around who really can read.

Fred can always think of something that might match the words Gina shows him!

But Fred is a little worried about September, when big school starts. Because he has already read Gina the reading book they'll be learning from in the first class. From page one right to the end.

And Fred is not one hundred per cent

sure that the stories he made up to go with all those lines of words are really the same as the stories in the reading book.

2. Fred Moves In with Grandma

Fred has a grandma. Grandma is Fred's Dad's mother. Grandma is seventy years old, a bit fat, and rather short. If you pinch her bottom with two fingers it wobbles like vanilla cream pudding. Or chocolate cream pudding, depending on whether Grandma is wearing a yellow skirt or a brown skirt.

Fred is very fond of his grandma. Dad and Joe are very fond of Grandma too. Mum is not quite so fond of Grandma, because Grandma never seems to like the things Mum cooks. And Grandma once said Mum didn't keep the flat clean; and she doesn't like Mum's tinted hair. Nor does Grandma approve of Mum going out to work. And, altogether, it seems as if Grandma would rather have had a different daughter-in-law.

Grandma used to live in the Old Market, just around the corner from the block of flats where Fred lives. Fred used to go and see Grandma almost every day.

If he didn't like what was for supper at home, he used to say, "I'm going to supper with Grandma!"

If Mum wouldn't tell him a story, he used to say, "I'm going round to Grandma's for a story!"

And if Joe was unkind to him he used to go and see Grandma. For a bit of comfort. And if he was bored he used to go and see Grandma. To play. Grandma

didn't have real toys. When he went round to her place he played with playing cards, and chessmen, and buttons. And the china figures out of her glass-fronted cabinet.

But now Fred can't go to see Grandma when he want a nicer supper, or a story, or a bit of comfort, or when he's bored. Because Grandma has moved into an old people's home.

Every other Sunday Fred goes visiting with Dad and Joe. Grandma has her own room in the home, with a balcony and a bathroom and a tiny kitchen, where she can make herself a cup of tea. She has her meals in the dining room. She watches television in the television room. She plays cards in the games room. And every morning she gets medicine for her diabetes from the doctor's room.

Fred enjoys visiting the old people's home. All the old people like him. While Dad talks to Grandma, Fred goes to see Grandma's neighbours, the other old men and women who have rooms nearby. The ones who don't have any visitors on Sundays. He spends a few minutes in their rooms, telling them all kinds of things, and they give him chocolate or biscuits, or sometimes even a whole tin of sweets. The lady who lives on Grandma's left always has a box of Lego spares for Fred. She buys them specially for him.

But Fred doesn't visit the old men and women in Grandma's home for the presents. He visits them because he likes them, and because he knows they expect him every other Sunday.

*   *   *

One Saturday Fred was in a really bad mood. Things had started going wrong as soon as he got up.

Fred wanted to wear his red dungarees. But his red dungarees had disappeared. They weren't in the wardrobe, they weren't in the linen basket, and they weren't in the washing machine.

"Mum, I can't find my red trousers," said Fred, quite upset.

Mum just nodded. "That's right," she said. "I gave them to Steve. They were getting quite tight round your middle!"

Fred lost his temper then. How could Mum go giving away his favourite pair of red dungarees?

"You're beastly!" he shouted. "Get them back at once!"

But Mum wouldn't. "I'd be so ashamed, I'd die of embarrassment!" she said. "Steve's mother would think I was the meanest woman in the world!"

"But I want my dungarees back," yelled Fred. "I want them back this minute!"

And since Fred was so full of rage and fury, and all that rage and fury wanted to burst out of him somehow, he kicked the table leg. The table wobbled. So did the mugs on it.

"There's no need to behave like Rumpelstiltskin," said Mum.

Fred kicked the table leg again. Really hard this time. And this time the table

didn't just wobble: it shot right across the kitchen, and everything on it fell to the floor. The bread basket, the cups, the butter dish, the marmalade jar, the milk jug, the spoons and the knives. And the chairs all fell over.

"Get out of here!" cried Mum. "And stay out of my sight!"

She grabbed Fred and pushed him out of the kitchen.

Fred went into the bedroom to find Dad. Dad liked to sleep late on Saturdays. But he was awake by the time Fred came in.

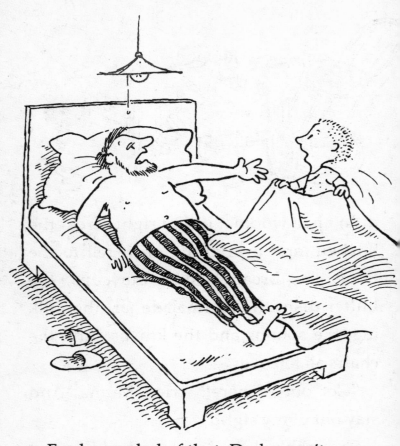

Fred was glad of that. Dad wasn't.

"Why are you squealing like a stuck pig?" said Dad crossly. "I'd like a bit more sleep!"

Fred wanted to tell Dad about the dungarees, and how unfair it all was, and he wanted to say he hadn't knocked all the things off the table on purpose. It wasn't his fault; his leg had just kicked out without his meaning it to.

But Dad pulled the covers over his head.

"Listen!" yelled Fred. "It's important!"

He pulled the covers back. Not just off Dad's head, but off the rest of him too.

Dad jumped out of bed. "Why on earth did I ever have children?" he shouted. And he marched out of the bedroom, slamming the door as he went. Fred was right behind him and the door handle hit him smack in the middle of the forehead.

Fred was totally fed up with his family!

He retreated to his own room in tears and put on his horrible new blue trousers. He decided to go and see Gina, but he met her and her Mum and Dad out in the corridor. Gina's Dad was just locking their front door.

"We're going to the supermarket," said Gina. "I'm going to buy a whole box of jelly babies. With the money Auntie Mary gave me."

"I'll come with you," said Fred.

"Sorry, no room," said Gina's Dad. "The car will be loaded up with crates of beer and mineral water and fizzy drinks!"

"There'll hardly even be room for Gina," added Gina's Mum.

Fred tugged Gina's sleeve. "Tell them

you'd rather stay here with me!" he whispered.

But Gina didn't want to. Gina loved going to the supermarket.

So Fred was fed up with Gina too.

But he didn't want to go home. Who wants to go home to a mother who's given away your favourite dungarees? Or to a father who rams a door handle into your forehead?

He couldn't hope for much from Joe either. Joe would only say, "Clear out, Titch!" or "Push off, Goofy!" Or, "Make yourself scarce, Twit!"

Fred stood in the corridor watching Gina and her parents go off and thinking, "Once upon a time I'd just have gone round to Grandma's. Those were the days!"

And then Fred thought, "I could still go round to Grandma's. It's easy. You just go straight down the High Street till you get to the big square with the railway bridge, and then along the street that goes off to the right. And then straight on till you reach the park. And then through the park. Past the roses and the jasmine and the fountain. And along the avenue. The old people's home is seven storeys high. You can't miss it."

Of course Fred knew he shouldn't simply go off like that. He knew he ought to tell his parents before going. But Mum had told him to stay out of her sight. And it was obvious to Fred that she wouldn't let him go off to see Grandma on his own.

He didn't want to tell Dad either. Well, the man had practically shattered his skull!

So Fred went off without a word. He set off down the High Street, walking as fast as he could. But although it had always seemed such a short journey in Dad's car, this time it dragged on and on – like the best sort of bubble gum. And Fred had a headache. He could feel a big bump on his forehead. He was hungry too. He hadn't eaten any breakfast. And he had no money for a bar of chocolate or a roll of fruit gums.

By the time Fred reached the railway bridge he was really tired. But it would be silly to turn back now, he told himself. He was sure he must have gone more than halfway.

So Fred carried on walking. He reached the old people's home at exactly twelve noon. He could tell from the big clock over the front door. Both hands were pointing straight upwards.

Fred crossed the hall and went up to the first floor. He realized how tired he was when he climbed the stairs! He could hardly pick up his feet.

On the first floor Fred knocked at the door saying Number 101. Then he shouted, "Grandma, it's me! Fred!" And then he tried the door handle. But the door was locked. Fred went to the next door along the corridor, knocked, and called, "Mrs Brown, it's me, Fred! Is my Grandma there with you?"

But the door of Room 102 was locked as well, and no one answered Fred.

He knocked at five doors. Without any luck. Until he reached the sixth: Mr

Martin was at home.

"All the old girls from the first floor have gone to the pictures," he said.

"Gone to the pictures at this time of day?" said Fred.

"No, I suppose not." Mr Martin scratched his bald head and thought about it. "Tell you what, I guess they're not back from Sunday service yet," he suggested.

"Sunday service on a Saturday?" asked Fred.

"No, that can't be it either!" Mr Martin scratched his tummy, a frown of concentration on his face. "Botheration," he muttered. "Darned if I can remember! They did tell me where they were going at breakfast. But my old brain's like a sieve: everything just goes in one ear and straight out the other!"

"Can I wait for my grandma in your room?" asked Fred.

"Of course," said Mr Martin.

So Fred sat on Mr Martin's balcony. Mr Martin gave him a huge tin of sweets, and Fred ate them all. Then he played beggar-my-neighbour with Mr Martin.

At one o'clock Mr Martin's alarm clock rang.

"I'm so forgetful, you see," said Mr Martin. "I set it to remind me it's time for lunch."

And Mr Martin went off to have his

lunch, leaving Fred all on his own.

Fred was getting bored. Very bored.

The balcony belonging to the room next door was right next to Mr Martin's balcony. There was only a wooden wall no higher than Fred between the two balconies.

Fred thought that the fourth balcony along must be Grandma's. He decided to find out if he was right. So he climbed over the first wooden wall, the second wooden wall and the third. In fact the third balcony along turned out to be

Grandma's. Fred knew it by Grandma's red folding chair, and the windowbox fixed to the outside of the balcony. Fred

was so tired that he folded the red chair all the way back to make a bed of it, lay down and went to sleep. Of course Fred never usually slept in the middle of the day. He just needed a few minutes' rest because he was so tired after his long walk.

But Fred slept longer than a few minutes. He didn't wake up until the telephone rang in Grandma's room. Fred yawned and rubbed his eyes. The telephone went on ringing.

"Perhaps it's important," thought Fred. "Perhaps Mr Miller is calling." Mr Miller was a retired teacher, and Grandma often went to the pictures with him.

"Perhaps Mr Miller has bought cinema tickets," thought Fred.

The balcony door was standing ajar. Fred opened it, went over to the telephone and picked up the receiver.

Usually, Fred said "Hello" when he picked up the phone, but a few days ago Joe had said, "It's no good just saying 'Hello', you twit; you have to give your name."

Fred wondered which name to give. His own or Grandma's? His first name or her first name? Or better still, his surname, because, after all, it was Grandma's surname too?

Before Fred could make up his mind a voice screeched in his ear, "Is Fred there

54

with you? Fred's been missing since before breakfast." And then there was a sobbing sound on the line.

The voice and the sobs belonged to Fred's Mum.

Fred felt really touched. He was about to tell Mum that there was no need for her to cry any more, and that she could come and fetch him. But then Mum sobbed, "That stupid, pigheaded child! He was carrying on like a lunatic this morning!"

Fred instantly stopped feeling touched! Pigheaded! Carrying on like a lunatic! That really was the limit. If Mum was going to talk about him that way, let her go on sobbing!

Fred decided to imitate Grandma's voice. Grandma had a funny habit of saying things twice. It was easy to imitate. So Fred said into the telephone, "Yes, yes, my dear, my dear! Fred has come to live with me, live with me from now on, now on! Because you're so nasty to him, so nasty to him!"

Fred thought he did it very well. He had even imitated Grandma's deep growl.

Unfortunately, Mum was even better at recognizing voices than Fred at imitating them.

"Fred!" she shouted down the phone and Fred hung up in a hurry.

Ten minutes later Mum and Dad were outside Grandma's door. They must have driven like the wind. They banged on the door and called for Grandma. And then they called Fred's name.

But Fred couldn't open the door. It was locked. Fred didn't want to open it, either. He was very cross with Mum and Dad.

So he climbed back over the wooden walls between the balconies again. But unfortunately Mr Martin's balcony door was now closed and locked. So were the

other balcony doors. Even Grandma's, as Fred discovered when he went back again. It must have clicked shut and locked itself behind him.

Fred was feeling terrible by now.

First he cried quietly, then he cried noisily, then he bawled the place down! But Mum and Dad didn't hear him. They were hammering on Grandma's door so hard, and shouting so loudly, that all they could hear was their own hammering and shouting.

However, there were people in the park down below, and they heard Fred all right. They saw him too. They fetched the caretaker and the caretaker went for an extending ladder and got Fred down from the balcony.

Just as Fred and the caretaker stepped down on to firm ground again, Mum and Dad came running out of the building.

Dad was going to be cross with Fred and so was Mum, but the man and woman who had fetched the caretaker said, "Now, now, don't be cross! Just be glad you have the lad back safe and sound! Why, he could have fallen and broken his neck!"

Mum and Dad saw the sense in that. And they really were glad to have Fred back.

Fred was glad too.

Since then Fred has given up the idea of moving in with Grandma at the old people's home.

It seems that life isn't so easy there either.

HELLO, FRED

Read more stories about Fred, his family and his friends in **Hello, Fred**.

Fred has a problem. Because he has lots of curly blonde hair, bright blue eyes and a rosebud mouth, people often mistake him for a *girl*! When a snooty new boy in the neighbourhood refuses to believe that he really is a boy, Fred decides it's time to take drastic action . . .

Storytime
from Play School

edited by Sheila Elkin

illustrations by Maureen Williams

Piccolo Original
Pan Books and the BBC

First published 1974 by Pan Books Ltd,
Cavaye Place, London SW10 9PG
and The British Broadcasting Corporation,
35 Marylebone High Street, London W1
6th printing 1981
© British Broadcasting Corporation and the Contributors 1974
ISBN 0 330 23824 8 (Pan) ISBN 0 563 12639 6 (BBC)
Printed in Great Britain by
Richard Clay (The Chaucer Press) Ltd, Bungay, Suffolk

STORYTIME FROM PLAY SCHOOL

Also published in Piccolo

More Stories from Play School
edited by Sheila Elkin

Contents

The Old Road

J. M. SMITH-WRIGHT

The old road was rough and stony and full of holes. Whenever it rained, the holes turned into big puddles and the stones became slippery, so it wasn't surprising that everyone in the town called it Mud Lane. Most of the houses at the top of Mud Lane had been pulled down long ago to make another road called New Road.

New Road had pavements on each side, trees with wire netting round, a shiny red letter box, and tall posts made of concrete with orange lights at the top. New Road and all the other roads in the town had their names at each end written in big black letters on a white background, so that everyone could read them. They had important-sounding names like *Lime Avenue* or *Frinton Rise*, but Mud Lane didn't have a name anywhere.

At the top of the lane where it joined New Road, there was one big building left – the school. One night, smoke started drifting across Mud Lane. There was a loud crackle of flames and the sky was red. Shouts filled the night. The school building had caught fire. Sirens sounded all over the town, followed by the shrill bell of the fire engine. Perhaps the fire engines would use the lane, as it was the shortest way, and New Road was blocked with traffic.

Suddenly, with a rumble and a whoosh, with sirens screaming and bells clanging, a shiny new fire engine rushed up Mud Lane – then another – then another.

They got to the school just in time. The fire was put out and the school buildings were saved.

A few days after the fire, some men came with a

large red notice and put it right across Mud
Lane.

It said: ROAD CLOSED.

Perhaps Mud Lane was going to be closed for
ever! But later that day the men came back with

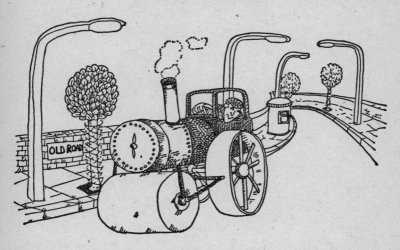

great lorries and a steamroller. They cut down all
the old hedges. They filled up all the holes with
grit, put pavements on both sides of the road, and
neat walls. They planted trees and put wire netting
all round.

Other workmen came to put up tall orange
lights, and there was even a shiny red letter box.

But best of all, when the men had quite finished,

they brought two boards, and put one at the top and one at the bottom, so that all the people in the town could read the name in big black letters on a white background: OLD ROAD.

Mud Lane was a road at last.

Farmer Cake and Farmer Rake

JUDITH MILES

Once, a long time ago, two farmers lived on the
same farm, in a round farmhouse with a red roof.
All around the farmhouse there were green fields,
and sheep and cows.

One of the farmers was called Farmer Cake. He was fat – his face was very round, and his blue eyes twinkled when he laughed.

The other farmer was called Farmer Rake. He was so thin he could dance and turn cartwheels all day and never feel tired. His face was long, and his blue eyes twinkled when he laughed. Both farmers laughed and sang all day long.

Farmer Cake sang:

> 'Oh, I am happy Farmer Cake
> I live on buns and chocolate cake;
> I'm big and round and fat and gay,
> I sing my happy song all day.'

Farmer Rake sang:

> 'Oh, I am happy Farmer Rake
> I do a handstand when I wake;
> I'm thin and light and quick and bright,
> I sing my happy song all night.'

Although fat Farmer Cake and thin Farmer Rake looked so different, they were very good friends. 'This parcel is for you, Farmer Cake,' said Farmer Rake. 'It's your birthday today.'

'No, this parcel is for you, Farmer Rake,' said Farmer Cake. 'It's your birthday today, too.'

'So it is,' they both said together. 'It must be a present for both of us.' They unwrapped the parcel and lifted out a beautiful blue velvet jacket with silver buttons down the front.

'You will look very good in this jacket, Farmer Rake,' said Farmer Cake. 'You must wear it on Sunday.'

'No,' said Farmer Rake, 'you will look much better in it than I will. *You* must wear it on Sunday.'

'We will both wear it on Sunday,' they said together.

'You shall wear it in the morning,' said Farmer Rake, 'and I shall wear it in the afternoon.'

When Farmer Cake put the jacket on, it was much too tight, and wouldn't do up.

When Farmer Rake put the jacket on, it was much too big. So Farmer Cake said: 'I'm not going to eat another thing until I am thin enough to wear this blue velvet jacket with the silver buttons!'

And Farmer Rake said: 'I'm going to sit and eat so that I grow big enough to wear this blue velvet jacket with the silver buttons!'

So Farmer Rake ate buns and chocolate cake and stopped doing handstands; and Farmer Cake tried to do handstands and stopped eating buns and chocolate cake.

Farmer Cake got very tired and hungry and cross – but he didn't get any thinner.

Farmer Rake got very ill and uncomfortable and cross – but he didn't get any fatter.

Soon the two farmers stopped singing. They didn't pick the apples and they didn't dig the potatoes. They didn't milk the cows and they

forgot to feed the pigs. And still the blue velvet jacket with the silver buttons down the front hung in the cupboard.

Farmer Cake got hungrier and hungrier, and Farmer Rake got more and more ill. At last Farmer Rake and Farmer Cake both spoke together: 'You will look much better than I will in the jacket – you wear it!'

Then Farmer Cake and Farmer Rake burst out laughing and Farmer Cake sang:

> 'I am merry Farmer Cake,
> I'd rather laugh and eat and bake,
> Or make a picnic lunch and pack it,
> Than wear any velvet jacket.'

and Farmer Rake sang:

> 'I am merry Farmer Rake,
> I'll do cartwheels till I ache,
> I'd rather laugh and make a racket,
> Than wear any velvet jacket.'

So Farmer Rake and Farmer Cake took the blue jacket with the silver buttons down the front and hung it on a pole.

'Now we have a scarecrow,' said Farmer Cake.

'It fits the scarecrow better than us,' said Farmer Rake.

They put the scarecrow in the middle of the dark brown field where they grew their cabbages and potatoes.

It kept all the birds away from the fields. Farmer Cake and Farmer Rake grew so many more cabbages and potatoes that they made their fortunes. Each of them bought a beautiful blue velvet jacket with silver buttons down the front. A small narrow one for Farmer Rake, and a big wide one for Farmer Cake, and they laughed and sang more than ever.

The Three Pomegranates

URSULA DANIELS

Once there was an old man called Ben who lived alone in a small cottage. On the kitchen table in the cottage he kept an empty bird-cage. It had not always been empty. Not long before, a sparrow had lived there while his broken wing got better. Then he flew away to join the other sparrows. Ben still missed the happy sound of chirping that used to fill the kitchen. Often he sat at the kitchen table staring sadly at the empty bird-cage.

One day he decided to cheer himself up. He went to the greengrocer's and bought a pomegranate as a special treat. It was round, about the size of a large orange, and it had a hard, reddish skin. He brought it home and laid it down on a plate on the kitchen table. Just as he was about to cut it in half so that he could eat it more easily, a tiny head popped out of the top.

'Goodness! What's that?' Ben exclaimed, peering closely. A very small caterpillar crawled out. When he saw Ben staring at him, he slid back in again. 'All right, all right!' Ben murmured gently. 'If this is your home, you can keep it,' for he was a kind-hearted man.

He left the pomegranate on the plate and went back to the greengrocer's to buy another one.

While he was away, his grandson William called to see him. William's eyes lit up when he saw the pomegranate on the table. 'Ooh, that looks nice,' he said. 'I'm sure that grandpa wouldn't mind if I ate just half of it.' So William cut the pomegranate into two pieces and ate one of them.

When Ben returned, he was horrified to see what William had done. He looked hard, and breathed a sigh of relief. The caterpillar was still there. William had eaten the bottom half of the pomegranate. 'You can't like being indoors,' said Ben to the caterpillar. 'I'm sure you need some fresh air.'

So he put the half-pomegranate on the plate on the window-sill beside an open window. The caterpillar felt the warm sunshine on his back.

But soon a huge blackbird hopped onto the window-sill. He spotted the juicy pomegranate, and with a toss of his strong beak he turned it over and pecked greedily at the fruity inside. Ben was just going to cut open the second pome-granate that he had bought when a loud noise drew him to the window. The blackbird was eating so fast that the plate was banging up and down.

In the nick of time, Ben rushed across the room making a hissing 'shoo-shoo' sound and the blackbird flapped hastily away onto the lawn. 'Perhaps that wasn't such a good idea after all,' Ben thought, as he carefully searched what was left of the pomegranate. At last he saw the cater-pillar wriggling on the plate. He had crawled out of the pomegranate.

Ben picked him up and took him over to the

table. 'I don't think I'm ever going to get a pomegranate eaten,' he sighed, lifting the caterpillar onto the second pomegranate. 'This can be your new home. You burrow a hole in there while I go out and buy myself another pomegranate.'

Then he had a thought. The little caterpillar had already had three narrow escapes. First Ben had nearly eaten him; then William, then the blackbird. How could he be sure that the caterpillar would be safe this time? Ben looked around and saw the empty bird-cage on the table. 'That's it!' he said.

He placed the pomegranate and the caterpillar inside the cage. In the kitchen drawer he found a padlock which he used to lock the cage door. 'Now you're quite safe,' he beamed. 'No one can reach you, but if you ever want to get out, you're small enough to climb between the bars.'

He put the key in his pocket and set out to buy a third pomegranate – this one really for himself. The greengrocer was rather surprised to see Ben again so soon.

But not nearly as surprised as the neighbours were when they discovered that Ben kept a pomegranate in his bird-cage. You see, Ben told no one about his new friend. It was a secret. And no one ever looked hard enough at the pomegranate to see that a tiny caterpillar was hiding there. But Ben knew that one day there would be one more beautiful butterfly, because he'd saved a caterpillar.

Pick Up a Pin

RUTH CRAFT

One day Janet was out walking with her Gran when she saw something bright and shiny on the ground. It was a pin!

'You want to keep that,' said Janet's Gran. 'It's lucky. People say: "See a pin and pick it up, and all the days you'll have good luck!"' So Janet picked up the pin and pinned it behind her coat collar.

It didn't seem to bring her any special luck, but Janet went on picking up pins all the same,

23

and putting them in her collar. She soon had several rows of pins.

But nothing especially lucky happened to her.

Then, one Saturday morning when she was on her way back from getting some shopping for her mother, she passed a church. There were a lot of people outside; they looked as if they were waiting for something, so Janet stopped and waited too.

In a minute a big, black, shiny car came along, and out of it stepped a beautiful bride. She had a long white dress on, and a long floating veil; she smiled at everybody and looked very happy.

But as the bride moved away from the car there was a ripping sound. The edge of the long dress had caught on the wheel of the car and there was a tear in it!

The bride was very unhappy – she wouldn't go into the church for her wedding in a torn dress, and nobody had a needle and thread.

Suddenly Janet remembered her pins. She took them all out and gave them to the bride to pin the tear in her dress together.

Now you couldn't see it had ever been torn!

The bride was very happy, and she asked Janet

to come to a special party after the wedding, in
the church hall.

Janet ran home to tell her mother and put on her
best dress. It was a marvellous party: there were
jellies and trifle and sausages on sticks to eat, and
an enormous wedding cake – and a band played
for people to dance.

That night, after the party, Janet's Gran said:
'There you are, that was a bit of luck! Lucky for
the bride you came along with your pins – and
lucky for you to have that nice party to go to!'

Josh Jolly and the Flag

JOYCE TOMSETT

Mr Josh Jolly had a very important job. He lived in the top of the tower of Calimba Castle, and it was his job to watch all the roads leading to the castle. If he saw the butcher or the grocer coming, he told the cook. If he saw strange soldiers, he told the Captain of the Guard; but if he saw the King coming, he had to fly the King's own flag from the top of the castle tower.

This flag was only flown when the King was at home. It was dark blue and yellow with orange stars.

Now the King was not often at home. He was

always fighting a battle somewhere or other, so Mr Josh Jolly didn't have to worry about the flag very often. This made him a bit lazy.

One warm summer's day, Mr Josh Jolly was just thinking about sun-bathing or having a sleep in a deck chair, when suddenly he heard the sound of trumpeters in the distance.

'How silly,' he said, 'I thought I heard the King's trumpeters – I must have been dreaming.'

Mr Josh Jolly stood up and looked. Coming towards the castle was a long procession, and right in the middle of it was the King.

'My goodness, nothing is ready! The flag! Where is the flag? The cook must be told. Where's the cook? Two hundred for dinner and no warning! The flag, the flag. WHERE'S THE FLAG? I must find it. The King will be cross if his flag isn't flying when he gets to the castle!'

Mr Josh Jolly dashed down the steps of the tower shouting: 'The flag is missing! The King is coming! Warn cook!'

He was so hot and bothered that by the time he reached the bottom of the steps he was saying: 'The flag is cooking! The cook is flagging! Warn King!'

He ran onto the castle lawn, and stopped and stared.

The royal children were playing there, and what were they using for their tent? Nothing else could be blue and yellow with orange stars! Quickly Mr Josh Jolly gathered the tent in his arms.

And just as the King came riding in through the castle gates, the flag fluttered from the top of the tower. Mr Josh Jolly was just in time – but there was something wrong. He took a closer look at the flag. He hoped the King wouldn't notice that the children had painted green dots all round it.

Just then the King sent for him. 'Now I'm for it,' thought Mr Josh Jolly. 'Now I'm for it.'

'Good morning, Mr Josh Jolly,' said the King. 'I see you are flying my flag.'

'Yessss . . . ssss . . . sir!'

'And I see you've changed it.'

'Yess . . . ss . . . sir!'

'I'm very pleased,' said the King.

'I think you have made it look much nicer. I've always wanted a flag with green spots round it. And I'm going to reward you. Arise – Sir Josh Jolly!'

And that's how Mr Josh Jolly became Sir Josh Jolly. He was never caught napping again, and always had the King's flag flying in good time.

Fearless Fred and the Jumble Sale

LIONEL MORTON

Fearless Fred the lion was walking through the village when he spotted a notice. It read:

GRAND JUMBLE SALE
SATURDAY AFTERNOON
BRING ALL YOUR JUMBLE

'Mmm,' thought Fred, 'that sounds interesting. I've a few old things at home I don't really want any more, and if I bring them here on Saturday afternoon I might see something I really need.'

So Fred set off for home.

On his way he met Harry the hippopotamus and told him about the jumble sale. 'Sounds like a good idea,' said Harry. 'I could bring this little stool I've got. It's much too small to sit on and it's very uncomfortable.'

'OK,' said Fearless Fred, 'I'll see you at the jumble sale on Saturday afternoon,' and off he went.

Well, Fearless Fred hadn't gone very far when he felt a few spots of rain and the wind began to blow – *shshsh* – and suddenly he saw something hurtling towards him. It was a huge, gaily-coloured umbrella, and clinging to the handle was Ronnie the rat.

'That umbrella's a bit big for you, Ronnie rat. Why don't you bring it to the jumble sale on Saturday afternoon? You might find something a bit more your size.' And off went Fearless Fred.

A bit further on his way he saw Ollie the ostrich coming towards him, looking very awkward and uncomfortable on a tricycle. 'Hey,' shouted Fearless Fred, 'are you coming to the jumble sale on Saturday?'

'Yes I am,' said Ollie, 'and I'm bringing this

32

wretched tricycle. It's most uncomfortable, and I have to push it up hills. I'll be only too glad to get rid of it.' And off he pedalled, wheezing and gasping.

Fearless Fred eventually got home and looked around for something he could take to the jumble sale. Then he spotted an old scooter. He had not touched it for ages, and it needed a good clean.

Saturday came, and Fearless Fred with his scooter, Ollie ostrich and his tricycle, Harry hippo and his tiny stool and Ronnie rat with his umbrella all bumped into each other on the way to the jumble sale. Harry hippo looked at Ronnie rat's umbrella. 'My, what a fine umbrella!' said Harry. 'Just what I need to keep me dry.'

'And that stool's just the right size for me,' said Ronnie. So they swopped.

Ollie ostrich looked at Fearless Fred's scooter. 'Ooh, I'd be so much more comfortable riding that! It's just the right size. Won't you swop my tricycle for your scooter?'

Fearless Fred looked at the tricycle. It did look rather smart. Ollie ostrich had polished it up, and it would certainly save his legs. So he agreed, and they swopped.

They were so happy with what they'd got there wasn't much point in going to the jumble sale, so they all went happily home. Ronnie had his stool, Harry the big umbrella, Ollie was pushing his scooter, and Fearless Fred was pedalling away furiously on his tricycle.

Tom's Kite

MALCOLM CARRICK

One day Tom set out to fly his kite in the park.

The kite was very pretty, with red and blue stripes, and ribbons on the string. It was so windy in the park that Tom soon had the kite flying. He held tight onto the string, letting it out more and more until the kite was far away in the sky.

Suddenly the wind changed, and the kite flew out of Tom's hand. It sailed over the lake and out of sight. Tom ran round the lake, trying to see where his kite had gone. It was not in the water, nor on the path, nor even on the grass. Tom sat down with a bump on the park bench.

'I've lost it now,' he cried. 'Oh, bother!'

'Pardon,' said a voice. It was the park-keeper, picking up paper with his pointed stick. 'What's all this, then?'

'I've lost my kite, park-keeper.'

'Is it red and blue with ribbons?' the park-keeper asked.

'Yes,' Tom said, 'but how did you know?'

'Well, it came whizzing over here and gave me a fearful surprise, and now it's up there.' The park-keeper pointed up to a tall tree, and there was the kite.

'Oh,' Tom cried, 'but how can we get it down?' The park-keeper tried to reach the string of the kite with his paper-picking-up stick, but it was no good. The park-keeper said he was very sorry, but Tom would have to wait until next week, when the tree cutters came with their ladders.

'That's no good,' thought Tom, as the park-keeper walked off. He sat down again. 'Oh, fish and chips!' he shouted. He always shouted that when he was very angry.

'Do you mind?' said a voice. It was a fisherman from the edge of the lake. 'You're scaring all the fish away, shouting "fish and chips" like that.'

Tom said he was sorry, and explained about his kite being caught in the tree. 'Well,' said the fisherman, 'as you've scared all the fish away with your crying, I'll get my fishing rod and fish for your kite.'

The fisherman brought his fishing rod from the lake and tried to poke the kite out of the tree, but it was just too high.

So he let out a little line and flicked the rod; and down came Tom's kite. 'It's a little battered and torn,' the man said, 'and you'll need some more string for it.'

'That's all right,' Tom laughed; 'next time I

fly it I'll tie the end of the string round my middle.'

'If it's as windy as today, I expect you'll fly off with it,' laughed the fisherman, 'and I couldn't fish *you* out of a tree, could I?'

Tom thanked the kind man who had saved his kite, and whenever he went into the park after that he walked around the lake to say 'hello' to the fisherman. But he said it very quietly, in case he scared the fish away.

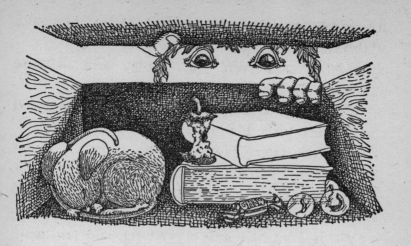

Tom's First Day at School

MALCOLM CARRICK

Tom was very happy because it was his birthday and his first day at school. His mum took him through the big gate, through the big playground with all its swings, into his classroom. 'Marmalade,' Tom said (he always said that when he was surprised). 'What a lot of things there are to do here!'

There was painting and water and sand, and soft squidgy stuff called clay, all on tables, and a nice teacher with a mini-skirt. 'Hello,' she said, 'I'm Mrs Maloney.'

'Hello,' said Tom. 'Can I play with all these things?'

The teacher said he could, and while Tom played with everything, his mum talked to the teacher.

'See you later, Tom,' said his mum; 'I won't forget your birthday present.' Tom waved to his mum, but didn't answer because he was too busy looking at the pets in his classroom's pets' corner.

When Tom had seen everything, and said hello to all the other children, Mrs Maloney showed him a desk where he could put his things. Tom lifted the lid, and there in the corner was a little mouse, fast asleep. 'Marmalade,' said Tom. 'Mum's got me a mouse for my birthday, and put it in my desk for a surprise.' He thought it seemed quite happy where it was, so he closed the desk lid very quietly, and went back to play. Suddenly there was a shout from one of the girls. 'Dilly's gone,' she shouted. Everybody rushed to the pets' corner.

Mrs Maloney looked worried. 'We must look everywhere,' she said, so Tom and all the children started looking for Dilly.

'Mrs Maloney,' Tom asked after a while, 'what does Dilly look like?'

'She's small and dark,' said Mrs Maloney. Tom ran off into the corridor, not sure what he was looking for. 'Small and dark and a she,' he thought. Then he saw a girl asleep on a bed.

'Are you Dilly?' he asked. 'Everyone's looking for you, you know.'

The girl opened one eye. 'Dilly is Mrs Maloney's mouse. My name is Sandra.'

'Oh, fish and chips,' Tom said suddenly, and rushed back into the classroom.

'Is Dilly a mouse?' Tom asked everyone.

'Yes, Tom, didn't you know?' Mrs Maloney asked.

'I think I know where she is,' said Tom, and he lifted up the lid of his desk.

'There's Dilly!' said all the children.

'I thought it was my birthday present,' Tom said sadly.

'I expect your mum will get you something else, Tom,' Mrs Maloney said, 'but never mind, you can look after Dilly, because you found her.' When Tom told his mum and dad all about the mouse and school, they were very surprised.

'We didn't know you wanted a mouse for your birthday, Tom; we've bought you a train.'

'That's all right, because I can look after the mouse at school, and have a train at home,' Tom said.

So Tom had a very happy birthday.

The Secret Present

JOHN YEOMAN

It was the afternoon of Vicky's birthday party. Simon had been looking forward to it and was in the hall, getting ready to go.

His mother did up his coat. 'Have you got your gloves, Simon?' she asked. Yes – they were tied to his wrists with elastic. And a handkerchief. And Vicky's present – the pair of tartan socks?

No! Simon had forgotten Vicky's present. Off he ran to his room to look for it. There was the package, wrapped in gaily striped paper, next to his cage of pet white mice.

'What a good idea,' thought Simon. 'I'll give

Vicky one of my mice as well, as a *secret* present. I've got plenty.' And he put the smallest mouse in his pocket.

When Simon arrived at Vicky's house and had said 'Hello' to everybody, he gave Vicky her real present – the tartan socks. Just as he was going to whisper to her about the other present, his secret present, the white mouse jumped out of his pocket and scampered off into the next room where the other children were playing party games.

'Oh! What was that?' cried Vicky. 'It looked like a mouse.'

'It *was* a mouse,' said Simon. 'And it's your secret present. Let's go and catch it.' And they both ran into the other room to try to find the white mouse.

The other children were playing 'Pin the tail on the Donkey'. Vicky's mother was blindfolding each of the children in turn, and they were all having a go at trying to pin a tail onto a drawing of a donkey. While they were doing this, Vicky and Simon looked for the hidden white mouse. But it wasn't in the tall green vase, and it wasn't down the side of the armchair.

Then Vicky's mother suggested a game of

'Blind Man's Buff'. She again blindfolded each of the children in turn, and they had to catch someone and guess who it was. This gave Vicky and Simon another chance to look for the white mouse. But it wasn't in the record player, and it wasn't in the ash-tray.

After that, they played 'Musical Chairs'. Vicky's mother played a tune on the piano while the children walked round a row of chairs. When the music stopped, everyone had to try to find a seat. While this was going on, Vicky and Simon had another look for the white mouse. But it wasn't in the doll's house, and it wasn't in the waste-paper bin with the pink roses on the side.

The last game of all was 'Hunt the Thimble'. Vicky's mother hid her thimble somewhere in the room, and all the children had to try to find it. So while the other children were all busy looking for the thimble, Vicky and Simon were searching for the white mouse.

They looked everywhere. And they were just beginning to think that they would never find it when – what do you think happened?

Simon saw one of the tartan socks, which he had given Vicky as a real present, give a slight

twitch. When he picked it up, there inside it was the little white mouse.

They were delighted to find the mouse again, and Vicky thanked Simon for his surprise present. And the mouse had its share of cake–crumbs to eat.

At last it was time to go home. Everyone agreed that it had been a wonderful birthday party, and Vicky whispered to Simon that his white mouse was the best birthday present she had ever had.

Raggy Maggy

BARBARA STONES

Raggy Maggy was Susie Simpson's rag doll, and a present from Susie's aunty Kate. Her face was made of pink silk with buttons for eyes. This gave her a surprised look, and so all that happened to her – from having porridge for breakfast from Susie's plate, to riding on the back of Susie's tricycle round the garden – made her look surprised.

One day Susie dressed Maggy in her dress with pink stripes, because her mother said they were going to town on the bus to buy Susie some shoes. Her mother had her basket and purse, and Susie picked up Raggy Maggy and off they went.

Soon the bus came along. And Susie lifted Maggy, and her mother lifted Susie, into it. They decided to go upstairs, because Susie hadn't been on the top of a bus before. They jogged along looking at the houses and gardens and then at the shops. Soon the conductress came to sell them their tickets, and Mummy gave them to Susie to hold. Susie thought it was great fun to travel on the top of the bus.

Suddenly her mother said, 'Come along, we must get off. Here is the market place.' Quickly they started to get off.

The bus started off again with a jerk, and what do you think? There was Raggy Maggy, looking more surprised than ever, sitting all by herself in the bus.

It wasn't very interesting, really, because Maggy was only small, and although Susie had propped her up on the seat she wasn't big enough to see out of the window. The bus went on and on, taking her further all the time from home. 'I wish Susie would come back,' she thought.

Then the old man who was sitting behind Raggy Maggy got up. He looked very surprised when he saw Raggy Maggy. 'I'd better take her to the conductress,' he thought, and he took her downstairs. He had picked Maggy up by her legs so that her head and the top half of her body flopped over backwards and she saw everything in the bus upside down.

The conductress put Maggy in a little cupboard under the stairs so that she would be safe. Maggy didn't like that very much, but soon they got to the bus garage. The cupboard was opened and Raggy Maggy was taken out of the cupboard and across the yard to the Lost Property Office, where she was put down on the counter. She had quite an exciting day watching everyone coming and going at the bus station.

When Susie discovered that she'd left Raggy Maggy on the bus she was very upset, but she cheered up when Mummy said that when they had finished their shopping they would go to the bus garage.

They arrived there in the afternoon, and soon

found the Lost Property Office. The man behind the counter said he would have a look and see if Raggy Maggy had been handed in; and sure enough, there she was in among all the umbrellas and parcels that other people had left on buses.

'Is this Raggy Maggy?' he asked.

It was. Then Mummy signed a book to say that she had got Raggy Maggy safely back.

'Raggy Maggy, Raggy Maggy,' shouted Susie, and hugged her over and over again. Raggy Maggy was very happy too, and her eyes seemed to shine more than ever. Mummy took Susie to buy some sweets, and then they went home. But this time Susie held on to Raggy Maggy *all* the way.

Merrylegs

PETER WILTSHIRE

Andrew lived with his parents and brothers and sisters in a large house at the top of the hill.

His room was full of toys, but when he was small his favourite was a rocking horse. The rocking horse was called Merrylegs, and her name was painted in a gold scroll underneath her mane. Merrylegs was brown with white spots and a yellow mane. She was getting old now, as Andrew's brothers and sisters had all ridden on her before Andrew was born, and her mane was very ragged.

By the time Andrew came to ride on her the reins and stirrup straps were broken, and the paint had rubbed off her sides.

Then one morning in the spring, Andrew's mother decided to turn out his room. 'Look at that old rocking horse,' she said. 'What a mess it looks! And you're much too big for it now, Andrew. Do you mind if I give it to the scrap-man when he calls?'

Andrew didn't mind, as he had plenty of other toys and he was too big to ride on old Merrylegs. So onto the cart with all the rubbish went Merrylegs. The cart was emptied at the scrap-yard, and there Merrylegs stayed, among battered chairs and chests, boxes and bedsteads.

People used to visit the scrap-yard, looking for old baths or bicycle wheels and all sorts of odds and ends, but they only laughed when they saw the old rocking horse standing in the middle of the yard.

Merrylegs stayed there with all the rubbish, and when it rained she got very wet. The rain washed off her paint, and the metal bits in her saddle and stirrups were all going rusty. When it was hot and sunny everything in the yard smelled, and the dust blew up into Merrylegs' eyes. Sometimes at night it was so cold that in the morning Merrylegs would be covered with a layer of frost. And all through the day she was banged and knocked as goods were moved about the scrap-yard, and she got more and more dirty and scruffy.

The scrap-man looked at Merrylegs every morning, gave her a pat and said, 'I expect someone will find a use for an old rocking horse one day, you'll see.'

And then one morning a man with a big hat came into the yard and said, 'One of our roundabout horses is broken. We're on our way to open the fair on the Green and we must have a new one. Don't suppose you've got anything like that, have you?'

'Oh,' said the scrap-man, 'I've got a rocking horse somewhere – but it's a bit old and it needs a coat of paint.'

'Never mind,' said the man when he saw Merrylegs, 'we'll soon paint it up and make a fine-looking roundabout horse.'

So he took Merrylegs and first he rubbed off all the rust. Then he painted her all over, with glossy brown and white paint. He gave her a new woolly

mane and two new, bright red reins, and last of all
he painted the golden scroll and her name 'Merrylegs' on the side of her neck. He got her ready just
in time for the fair on the Green, and fixed her on
the roundabout with the twisty, shiny pole coming
from her back. She spent all day going round and
round to the music of the merry-go-round with
children riding on her back – and she was happy.

A Duck called Donald

JOHN LANE

Donald the duck lived in a large garden. She didn't know why she was called Donald, because that is a boy's name, and she was a lady duck. Everyone called her Donald, so Donald it was. She didn't mind at all – in fact she rather liked it.

In the large garden was the duck house where she slept. It was a wooden house with glass windows which could be opened in the hot summer days to let the cool air in. In the winter when it was cold the windows were fastened tight shut. This made the duck house very snug and warm, particularly as the floor was covered in clean straw.

55

There were two other ducks in the duck house
Charlie the drake, a very handsome fellow wit
dark, greeny-blue feathers round his neck and
curly tail, and Ethel the Aylesbury, whose feather
were white. She was always in the water, washin
and cleaning herself. A bit of a bore, Donal
always thought. Donald was a Cookie Campbe
duck and had nice light-brown feathers whic
didn't need nearly as much cleaning as Ethel's.

Donald used to get up quite early every mornin
and go to an old iron bath which had fresh wate
in it. She would have a quick wash and then go fc
a walk round the garden. Her favourite spot wa
the rockery, where she could grub about for a
sorts of juicy worms and bugs underneath th
stones. It was quite easy to move the stones wit
her strong beak.

Another spot she liked visiting was the lila
bush. After she had finished grubbing about in th
rockery, she would waddle over the big stone
on her webbed feet and along the path towards i
It was quite a large lilac bush and in the summe
she would very often sit down right in the middl
where no one could see her, and watch anyone tha
happened to go along the path. It might be Fre

the cat, or Clover the dog. Or sometimes she'd just have a quiet think, or even drop off to sleep.

Well, one day Donald was in the rockery getting her breakfast when she tripped and fell over a rather large stone. Her foot did hurt and it began to swell.

The following day it was still very painful so she stayed a little longer in the iron bath. The water was cool and made her foot more comfortable but the swelling was still as bad.

For the next two or three days she hobbled slowly round the garden – sitting down very often to have a rest. Then, one morning she saw that Ethel the Aylesbury had laid a lot of eggs in the duck house, but was so busy washing herself she hadn't time to sit on them to keep them warm! Donald knew right away what she must do. She hobbled over to the nest and gently sat down over the eggs. It was so restful to be sitting down all day instead of trying to walk. The people whose garden it was brought her food. Every morning she would get up to have a quick wash and waddle back to the eggs in the nest.

Then one day Donald felt something move under her, and stood up. How exciting! One of the

eggs had cracked and a tiny bill was peeping out. As she watched, a second, third, fourth, fifth and sixth egg broke, and out scrambled six baby ducklings, small and yellow and fluffy.

The surprising thing was that with all that sitting down, her foot was better. So, next day, when she went off into the garden, she was followed by the six baby ducks.

Such a Useful Elephant

JOANNE COLE

Once upon a time there was a very small zoo in the country, with just one keeper. There were some goats ... some ducks ... lots and lots of rabbits, guinea pigs and hamsters ... two ponies, two donkeys ... and one elephant.

The keeper thought a lot of his elephant. 'Clever elephant, that,' he would say. 'Mark my word ... that's a clever beast, that elephant! You just have to see the look in his eye. Nothing like your ordinary clever elephant – much cleverer than that.' And Hugo (that was the elephant's name) would look at Kevin (that was the keeper's name), and Kevin would look at Hugo and say: 'I don't know *what* he's thinking but I know he *is* thinking.'

Apart from his animals, Kevin the keeper was very proud of the flowers in the zoo. Several times he had won prizes for the prettiest zoo, and bees often queued up to visit his flowers.

But one summer it was so hot and dry that all the flowers drooped and looked as if they were going to die. Kevin the keeper toiled away in the blazing sun to give his flowers water. One day it was so sunny and he was so tired that he did something he'd never done before.

He fell asleep on duty!

The butterflies fluttered, and the bees buzzed round his head, and Kevin the keeper snored gently in the sun.

When he awoke he reached for his watering can and noticed straight away that the rose – that's the bit on the end of the spout with holes in – had gone. Where could it be?

Then he saw that Hugo had taken it and had stuck it in the end of his trunk. 'Here, Hugo!' the keeper shouted.

But Hugo made off towards the duck pond.

When he reached the pond, Hugo lowered his trunk with the rose on the end into the pond and filled it with water. 'What's he playing at?' Kevin the keeper asked himself. 'What is that four-footed beast playing at! Come back!'

But Hugo didn't come back. He went trotting towards the flower beds. 'Oh, no!' said Kevin. 'He's going to squash all my flowers!'

But when he reached the beds the elephant trod *very* carefully between the flowers and, standing on one leg in the middle of the bed, he

began squirting water onto the flowers through the rose in the end of his trunk.

As soon as he ran out of water, he went back to the duck pond. He filled his trunk again and went on watering the flowers.

In no time at all the flowers were standing upright, and spreading their leaves and petals in the sunshine. Soon the air was filled with their scent.

Kevin was so delighted that he changed into his swimming trunks and had a cool shower from Hugo as the flowers were watered. 'Clever elephant, that,' said Kevin the keeper. 'Much cleverer than your *ordinary* clever elephant!'

A Goose called Fred

JEAN WATSON

Terry and his family lived on a farm where there were all kinds of animals. Terry liked all of them, but he had one special pet. It wasn't a dog, it wasn't a cat, it wasn't a fish in a tank. It wasn't even a mouse or a hamster.

It was a white goose called Fred.

Fred followed Terry everywhere. Now some geese are grumpy and bad-tempered. They hiss – *ssss* – *ssss* – *ssss* – to show they're cross.

But not Fred. He just honked a lot. He was

63

friendly with everybody and every animal on the farm.

One day Terry noticed that Fred wasn't anywhere in the house. 'Anyone seen Fred?' Terry asked.

'No,' said his mother. 'Perhaps he's talking to the ducks.'

So Terry went off to see. 'Fred! Dinner time!' he shouted. But all he could hear was *quack*! *quack*! from the ducks.

'Oh, I know,' said Terry. 'He's probably talking to the sheep.'

So he went to the field where the sheep were nibbling. 'Fred, Fred! Dinner time!' he shouted. But all he could hear was *baa*! *baa*! *baa*! not *honk*! *honk*! *honk*! and all he could see were white woolly backs – not a white feathery one anywhere. 'Oh, I know,' said Terry. 'He's probably with the cows.'

So he went to the field where the cows munched and mooed. 'Fred, Fred, dinner time!' shouted Terry. But all he could hear was *moo-moo*, and all he could see were large brown bodies – not a white waddly one anywhere.

'Perhaps he's with the horses,' said Terry, and

ran to the field where the horses stamped and champed.

'Fred, dinner time!' he shouted. But all he could hear was *phrr phrr* and all he could see were long legs and stamping hooves – not a pair of webbed feet anywhere.

'Oh, I know,' said Terry. 'Fred's probably with the pigs.' So he went to the field where the pigs were lying in the sand.

'Fred, Fred, dinner time!' he shouted. But all he could hear was *oink*! *oink*! *oink*! not *honk*! *honk*! *honk*! and all he could see were fat pink bodies – not a slim, white, tall one anywhere.

'There's only one more place he *can* be,' said Terry, 'with the hens!' So off he went to the hen run. 'Fred, dinner time!' he called. But all he could hear was *cluck*! *cluck*! *cluck*! and all he could see were red combs and brown feathers – not a sleek white head anywhere.

What if Fred had gone too far from the farm and got lost!

Terry started to run towards the house. He was so worried that he didn't even see the red post office van which had stopped outside the gate, until the postman climbed out and shouted:

'Hello, Terry! Come here a minute. I've a sort of parcel for you. Just wait while I get it out of the back, will you? It's a noisy parcel.'

'A noisy parcel!' cried Terry, wondering whatever could be in a noisy parcel. But it wasn't a brown-paper-and-string one at all.

It was Fred!

'Fred!' shouted Terry. 'I *am* glad to see you. I've been looking for you everywhere. How did you get into the van?'

'He must have flapped in while I was delivering parcels here earlier today,' said the postman. 'I

must have left the van door open. I didn't know he was there till I heard him honking.'

'Thank you for bringing him back,' said Terry to the postman.

'That's OK,' said the postman. 'Cheerio!'

'You silly goose,' said Terry to Fred, with a smile.

'Honk! honk! honk!' said Fred, and strutted back to the house as if nothing had happened.

The Jumping King

PETER WILTSHIRE

Once upon a time there was a king who wanted everything in a hurry.

'Jump to it!' he shouted all day long. 'Jump to it!'

If the footman was slow opening the door – 'Jump to it!' shouted the King in a fierce voice.

When the cook was late with his dinner the King banged the table and shouted, 'Jump to it, Cook – where's my dinner?'

Soon everybody in the palace was jumping to it. All of them jumped all the time at everything they did and soon so many people were shouting: 'Jump to it!' that the whole country was jumping about. They jumped out of bed in the morning and jumped back in again at night. The children jumped all the way to school, the shopkeepers jumped to serve their customers, and as for the King's councillors, they never stopped jumping long enough to think at all. The King became known as King of Jump Land. One year, when the royal birthday was near, he announced that there would be a big prize for the person who could jump higher than the King.

The people practised for weeks jumping up and down – higher and higher. And the palace began to shake with the bumping and banging.

The King called his councillors to the throne room – and they all came jumping in to see what the King wanted.

'Jump to it!' shouted the King, 'and listen.' He was beginning to get quite rude. 'Nobody is allowed to jump higher than me,' he said. 'Go and find a shoemaker who can make shoes for me to jump in, and jump to it!'

On the King's birthday hundreds of people had come from all over the Kingdom to compete

or the prize. Some had rubber socks on, some had
prings on their feet, and they jumped up and
down the courtyard while the bands played.
The King just sat and watched. Then he called
or silence, and announced that he was going to
ump. The councillors brought the King the pair
f special shoes.

'Here are the best jumping shoes, made by the
nest shoemaker in the land, Your Majesty.'

He put on his new shoes, the trumpets played,
nd the King jumped once – he jumped so high

that he went right across the courtyard. Then he jumped again, and his second leap took him over the massive walls and outside the palace grounds. The people waved and cheered – surely nobody could jump higher than that! Then the King jumped again, higher than ever, and suddenly he shot into the air like a rocket and flew off up into the sky until he disappeared.

The people gasped and courtiers gaped, but as no one said 'Jump to it!' they were still for the first time for months. They stood looking up waiting and waiting for the King to come down again. And suddenly he appeared at last and landed with a bump.

And he never shouted 'Jump to it!' to anyone ever again.

The Jug

JOANNE COLE

Long ago there lived a king who had a beautiful daughter. She was called Princess Smiling Face because she was always smiling.

When she grew up so many different men wanted to marry her, the King found it very difficult to choose between them. You see, in those days Princesses couldn't marry anyone they liked – they had to marry the man their parents liked. So the King hit on an idea. Anybody who wanted to marry the Princess had to give the right answer to a question the King would ask.

The King had a jug brought to him – an ordinary

brown earthenware jug. Everyone who came and wanted to marry the Princess was asked this question: 'Which is the most useful part of the jug?'

And not one of them could give him the answer he wanted. At last there were only three suitors left. They had travelled from far-off countries to the Princess's palace, and one was the richest, and one the bravest, and the other the cleverest man in the world.

'What is the most useful part of the jug?' the King asked again.

The bravest man in the world, a great general who had come with his whole army, picked up the jug, turned it over and over and said: 'The most useful part of the jug is the handle – without the handle you couldn't pick it up.'

'No,' said the King, 'next please.'

Next came the richest man in the world. He had arrived with a great caravan of wagons full of jewels. He looked at the jug a long time and then he said: 'The most useful part of the jug is the bottom. If the jug had no bottom all the water would fall out.'

'No,' said the King, 'next please.'

Next, and last, was the cleverest man in the world. He tapped the jug, listened to it, smelt it, felt it, and then said: 'The most useful part of the jug is the lip. Without the lip the water would pour all over the place.'

'No,' said the King.

Just then the man who had made the jug, who

had been in the palace while all this was going on, asked if he was allowed to answer the question. 'Certainly,' said the King, 'speak up.'

The potter took the jug and pointed inside it. 'The most useful part of the jug,' he said, 'is the empty bit inside. If it were not for that empty space inside there would be nothing to fill, and the jug couldn't hold anything.'

'Yes,' said the King. That was the answer he had wanted.

So the potter married Princess Smiling Face, and they lived happily ever after.

And what he said is true, isn't it? If it wasn't for the empty space inside the jug you couldn't fill it, could you?

Mischa the Museum Mouse

SHEILA FRONT

Mischa was a little mouse who lived in a museum. The museum was a beautiful old house with green lawns and trees and a round lake with swans on it.

Long ago, when Mischa's great-great-grandmother had lived there, the house had been the home of a rich gentleman and his family. But now the house was used as a museum, where old and interesting things were carefully preserved for people to look at and enjoy. There was a suit of armour at the foot of the staircase and many glass cases containing old coins, rare jewels and old-fashioned weapons. At the top of the wooden stairs was a large grandfather clock with a very loud chime.

Each day, when the museum was opened, an attendant in a dark blue uniform sat on a chair in the corner of the big hall to answer people's questions. At night time when everyone went home the attendant would carefully lock the museum doors and go home himself.

This was the time when Mischa's brothers and sisters scampered happily from their little hole in the wood panelling, and ran out to play in the gardens or the old stables.

But Mischa had a very different idea of fun. He liked to explore the museum and play games around the things he loved. He always found his supper under the attendant's chair. It was just a few crumbs from the man's sandwiches, but to Mischa it was a delicious snack. Then, when he was no longer hungry, Mischa happily ran all through the museum. He loved to swing on the pendulum of the great grandfather clock and would squeal with delight when the hours chimed.

On the walls were many fine paintings in carved olden frames. When Mischa was feeling tired he would sit down quietly and look at his favourite icture. It was a painting of a large piece of rich ellow cheese on a table. There were other things 1 the picture too, but Mischa only had eyes for he cheese. It looked so good that he felt sure he ould smell it.

When the morning light began to peep through he great windows of the house, Mischa would un to the safety of his little home in the all.

One night his adventures ended in a very dif-rent way.

As usual he came out to look for his supper, but, adly for Mischa, the attendant had been very areful with his lunch and had not left a single rumb. Mischa felt sad and hungry. He tried to rget his hunger by playing his usual games, but is heart was not in it.

At last he found himself sitting miserably by his vourite picture. As he looked up at the yellow, hellow cheese it became very tempting to him. His whiskers twitched and his eyes shone. He *must aste that cheese*. In a flash he had scampered up a

79

nearby hot water pipe and was perched on th
golden frame. A second later he was nibblin;
hungrily.

Although Mischa did not know it, behind th
picture ran a wire which could set off a burgla
alarm connected to the police station.

At exactly this time, in one of the other rooms
burglar wearing a mask and carrying a sack and
torch was quietly climbing through a window. H
crept to a glass case which contained some ver
valuable jewels and in a few moments he ha
managed to break open the lock. He opened hi

sack and plunged his hands greedily among the jewels.

At this moment Mischa had gnawed right through the canvas and his little nose touched the wire. The museum was suddenly filled with a jangling of bells. The loudest noise you can imagine filled the silent night. Mischa ran into a corner in fright and the burglar dropped the jewels and hurried to the window to escape. He only had one leg over the window ledge when the police cars arrived, and in no time at all the burglar was hand-cuffed and taken away.

Two important policemen began to search the museum to see if anything *had* been stolen and to find out who had set off the alarm. When they came to the picture of the cheese they stopped and stared at the hole. Then they looked into the dark corner where two bright, frightened eyes were looking up at them. To Mischa's surprise they weren't a bit cross about the spoilt picture. Instead one of them bent and gently picked up Mischa.

'What a clever mouse,' said the other policeman. 'Fancy calling the police and saving the jewels. I wouldn't be at all surprised to see you rewarded, little mouse.'

The policeman was quite right, for the next morning a large parcel arrived for Mischa. It contained an enormous piece of cheese just like the one in the picture, and quite enough for the whole mouse family to share.

The gentleman who brought it also had another surprise. He told Mischa that the next day he must dress in his smartest clothes, as the Queen wanted to present him with a medal.

When the next day arrived Mischa was up bright and early. He combed his whiskers and put on a shiny top hat that had belonged to his grand-father.

A large, black car, driven by a chauffeur, arrived at the museum to take Mischa to the Palace.

You can imagine how important the little mouse felt when at last he arrived at the Palace and was taken into the magnificent room where the Queen was sitting on her golden throne.

It was all just like a dream to Mischa, and almost before he knew what was happening he was being driven back to the big house where his family, friends and of course the attendant, were waiting to admire his handsome medal.

After that, life carried on much as before for

Mischa. In fact many people had forgotten all about his adventure.

One day, however, something happened that was always to remind people of the night when Mischa had helped to catch a burglar. The Mayor and Corporation came to unveil a large statue which had been erected in front of the museum. When the cord was pulled, the cloth fell off the statue, and there was Mischa the Museum Mouse holding his top hat and, of course, wearing his medal.

The Secret of the Mountain

ROSEMARY GRAHAM

Once there was a boy called Crispin who lived in a
village in the valley by the side of a big mountain.
Most of the year it was warm and sunny in the
valley, and the flowers grew bright and thick along-
side the stream which flowed down from the nearby
hills. Only in winter did the flowers disappear, and
even then the valley looked beautiful, for it
sparkled and twinkled with the snow that covered
it.

Crispin liked to take some sandwiches wrapped

up in a yellow cloth, and walk along the stream as far as he could, trying to find where it began high up in the hills. But he never managed to. He always finished his sandwiches long before he'd gone half-way, and by the time he'd gone three-quarters of the way, he was so hungry that he'd turn round and go home. Occasionally, he would find sticks on the path – Crispin would take these home to his mother, who thanked him and used them for the stove, which cooked their food and warmed their water.

These sticks were rather strange. In fact, even the cleverest old grandfathers in the village could not explain them. They just seemed to appear from nowhere. Some had even been found in the middle of the village square. Everyone was puzzled, and guessed at what they could be. Some thought they were a giant's matchsticks. But nobody *knew* any-thing about them except Crispin, and even he didn't know *what* they were – only where they came from.

He knew that they came from the mountain which soared into the sky on one side of the valley – and this is how he found out.

One day, while Crispin was sitting by the stream,

dabbling his feet in the water, he looked up at the mountain, wondering how high it was. And then it happened. Very quickly. A stick came whizzing down from the snow at the top of the mountain and landed PLONK! on the grass by Crispin's sandwiches. Crispin took the stick home to his mother, and began to think. He thought that one day – he didn't know when – one day he would climb to the top of the mountain to discover its secret.

It was in summer that the special day came. Crispin woke early and he knew at once that he was going to the top of the mountain. He raced off as soon as he could – with the sandwiches his mother had given him. The mountain shone in the sun and Crispin was so excited that he climbed halfway up the hill in no time at all. Then he ate his sandwiches and set off again towards the top. There were no paths, and the sides of the mountain became steeper. The flowers didn't grow this high, for the ground became rocky and there wasn't much soil.

Higher and higher Crispin climbed, slower and slower his legs moved, but he knew that he was nearly at the top, so he went on bravely. He tripped twice, once because he wasn't picking up his feet, and once over a stick because he wasn't looking properly. Crispin knew that he was very close to the secret.

Four steps more, round a rock, and there he found, right at the top of the mountain, a small circle of soft grass and buttercups. In the middle was a large bear licking the biggest pink lollipop Crispin had ever seen.

'Hello,' said Crispin.

'Hello' said the bear, and went on licking.

Crispin didn't know what to do, so as he felt rather tired after his long climb, he sat down at the edge of the grass and watched the bear. The lollipop was very big, but the bear's tongue was also big, and before long the delicious pink lollipop had disappeared.

The bear sighed, smacked his lips, and gently tossed the lollipop stick over his shoulder, down the mountain.

Crispin laughed and laughed, for now he knew the secret of the mountain. Then he remembered his manners, and told the bear why he was laughing.

The bear, whose name was Tom, didn't think it was very funny; but as he had nice manners too, he decided to laugh with Crispin. He liked Crispin,

who was the first boy he had met, and told him he was very welcome on the top of his mountain. Crispin thanked Tom, and they shook hands and paws and became firm friends. Then Crispin said he must go home or his mother would worry, waved goodbye and set off down the mountain.

Very soon Tom disappeared from sight, and it was hard for Crispin to believe that he really had discovered the secret of the peculiar sticks.

When he reached home, Crispin told his mother and father all about his adventure on the mountain, and how he had found Tom the bear.

'Fiddlesticks!' said his father.

'No, LOLLIPOP sticks!' said Crispin.

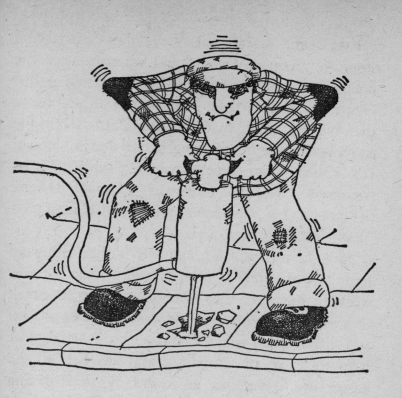

Trevor Bill the Road Mender

RUTH CRAFT

Once there was a very bad-tempered road mender called Trevor Bill. He snapped and growled and moaned at everybody. The only thing he liked was his job.

Every time he smashed up an old piece of paving stone he growled 'Grrrh,' and when he used the pneumatic drill he joined in the noise 'Gggrrhh! Gggrrhh!' But what he liked best of all was using that big clumping machine that flattens out the earth before the new paving stones are put down. It's called a pneumatic presser, and it goes *hurrumph*, CLUMP! *hurrumph*, CLUMP! Using the pneumatic presser was the job bad-tempered Tevor Bill liked best of all.

Now the men who worked with Trevor Bill were fed up with him. It was all right when he was working, but when they were having their tea break he was a terrible nuisance. It wasn't as if he just sat and sulked – that wouldn't have been so bad, but he used to sit in the little hut and snarl at all the passers-by. 'Walking all over my new paving stones! Treading all over my cement! Gggrrhh!' And then there would be quarrels and arguments and it was all very unpleasant. So they had a meeting among themselves and decided to try and improve his ways.

The next morning one of the men said to him: 'Ahem . . . excuse me, Trevor Bill, it's about your bad temper. Perhaps you could cure it by having an xtra cup of tea in the morning before you come to work?'

'There's nothing makes my temper worse than xtra cups of tea,' roared Trevor Bill.

'Perhaps,' suggested one of the men, 'you could ry growing flowers on your window-sill at home? Flowers are very good for bad tempers.'

'I hate flowers and I hate window-sills! Now will ou let me get on with my work?' snarled Trevor ill. And he stormed over to the pneumatic presser, icked it up and began going *hurrumph*, CLUMP! urrumph, CLUMP!

The workmen were in despair, but one of them houted over the noise to Trevor Bill, 'Well, you ould try singing while you work. That's very good or bad temper.'

During that morning a very strange thing appened. Instead of Trevor Bill just going Hurrumph, CLUMP!' he tried to *sing* '*Hurrumph* LUMP'! Then, when he was fetching the big ew paving stones from the pile and humping them o the flattened earth, he sang:

Oh, rum diddle dum, a bottle and a cork, There's nothing so solid as stones from York.'

The other workmen were amazed, and when it came to tea break, Trevor Bill was almost cheerful – he even offered to hand round the sugar. Lots of people passed by the hut and walked over the new

paving stones, and Trevor Bill didn't snarl at one of them.

Later on that morning, when they were all back on the road working away, Trevor Bill began to sing again:

'Oh mending roads for people like you,
To run and jump and walk on,
Is a very fine job which suits me well,

And I'd better get a move on.
Rum diddle dum, a bottle and a cork,
There's nothing so solid as stones from York.'

The people passing by stopped to listen. And when he'd finished they clapped politely and said: 'What a fine voice that road mender has,' and, 'What a pleasure to hear someone singing while they work.'

And Trevor Bill? Well, he was so pleased when he heard them say kind things about him that he smiled and went on singing louder than ever before. And from that day to this – as long as he's mending roads and singing at the same time, he keeps in a good temper.

The Giraffe who Loved Flowers

EILEEN MATHIAS

Once upon a time there was born in a country where the sun shines all day long and the jungle trees reach to the sky, a baby giraffe. His father and mother towered above him. They were almost as tall as the trees.

'You must stand up straight and look at the sky,' said his parents when he was quite young. 'Your food grows high up, the sweetest leaves are always at the top of the trees.'

But the young giraffe liked the flowers that grew

close to the ground far better than the leaves high in the sky. He smelt the flowers, he ate the flowers. He made flower chains to hang round his long neck and no one could understand how he felt about flowers, no one at all.

'You will have a crooked neck,' said his father.

'It will not grow straight if you keep on looking down at the ground,' echoed his mother. 'You will never grow up to be a tall, handsome giraffe like your father if you keep on looking down instead of up.'

But the little giraffe still kept on smelling the flowers. He ate them too.

'He should live in a park, not a jungle,' said his father.

'Yes,' agreed his mother, 'he should live in a park where there are beds full of flowers and not many tall, fine trees.'

The young giraffe, who was listening to their conversation, said to himself, 'Yes, that is where I must go – to a park. I could be very happy there amongst the flowers. I must go away from the jungle and find a park.'

So he went on his lollopy, wollopy way out of the jungle one summer day. He followed the scent of the flowers that grew by the road, because he thought that they might lead to more and more flowers in a park.

At last he reached the flat fields. A lion who had

just finished a good meal met him and said, 'I could eat you, young giraffe. I shan't because I'm not hungry, but aren't you afraid?'

'Not now that you've told me you've just had your dinner,' said the young giraffe. 'I'm on my way to find a park where the flowers grow. Can you tell me how to get there?'

'It's over there, a long way off,' said the lion, shaking his mane in the direction of the hills.

'Then I must be off,' said the young giraffe, 'and thank you for not eating me, and for telling me the way.' Off he went on his lollopy, wollopy way across the plains.

Then he met a leopard with her cubs. 'Where are you going to, young giraffe?' asked the leopard.

'To the park where the flowers grow, if I can find it,' said the young giraffe.

'Then be careful,' warned the leopard. 'I shan't eat you because I'm not hungry, but other creatures may.'

Away went the young giraffe on his lollopy, wollopy way. A ferocious-looking tiger came suddenly in sight. The young giraffe felt nervous for the very first time since he had left home, for the tiger had a hungry look in his eye.

'I'm on my way to find something for dinner,' said the tiger, eyeing the giraffe with interest, and then he took a closer look at him. 'But you won't do, because I don't like flowers with my food and you are wearing a garland of flowers round your neck. Where are you going, you silly young giraffe?'

'To the park where more flowers grow. I'm very fond of flowers. They're lucky for me.'

'Indeed, they are,' sneered the tiger. 'I don't like flowers in my dinner.'

Away went the young giraffe on his lollopy, wollopy way. He bent his head close to the ground. Yes, he could smell it. The scent came to him as he ran along with his head near to the ground and his clumsy young legs straddled and splayed out on either side of him.

On and on he went, and by the time morning came he had arrived. The scent of flowers in the park was so strong the little giraffe began to feel quite faint. He had never smelt so many flowers in his whole life before.

'I shall stay here for ever and ever. I shall hang flowers round my neck. I shall stay here until my neck is long enough to carry ten garlands of flowers.'

And he did stay until he was a full-grown giraffe, with a long, graceful neck that could bear ten garlands of sweet-smelling flowers. He was known far and wide, and his mother and father were content to leave him in the park of flowers for ever – he was so happy.

A Surprise for the King

MIKE ROSEN and ANNE REAY

Once upon a time there was a king who wanted
something special to happen on his birthday. So he
called all his courtiers together and said: 'This year
I want to have a real surprise for my birthday – not
just *ordinary* presents like gloves and hankies. What
I want is a real surprise.'

So everyone went away and thought about how
they could make the biggest surprise for the King.
The musicians went off to make surprise music, the
gardener went off to think about surprise flowers,

and the cook went off to think about surprise things to cook.

When the cook got home he told his wife all about the King's birthday. They sat down together to think about it.

'What about a picture of the King made out of icing?'

'No – we did that the year before last,' said the cook.

'What about a clockwork cake?'

'A clockwork cake? What do you mean?'

'A cake that moves.'

'You don't want cakes to move – you want them to stand still!' said the cook. 'We just don't know what to make for the King. We've made every sort of cake in the world.'

'I've got it!' said his wife. 'You must make *the biggest cake in the world*.'

'The very thing!' cried the cook. 'I'll make the biggest cake in the world.'

So the cook and his wife collected everything needed to make this huge cake. 'Here are the raisins,' said his wife. 'What else do we need?'

'Flour, butter, sugar, eggs, fruit, milk, nuts,'

said the cook. 'Heaps and heaps and heaps of it all. And we'll have to mix it in the bath.'

So they beat, and mixed, and began to stir it up.

Stir and stir and stir,
Stir and stir and stir.

When they had finished they put it into a huge pan, and because it was too big for any oven, they built a fire round it to bake it!

While it was baking, the cook went off to have his dinner, and he told his friends that he had made the biggest cake in the world. And his friends told *their* friends. And *their* friends told *their* friends and *their* friends, until very soon *everyone* knew about the biggest cake in the world and came to see it.

One by one they went up to the cake – it smelled so good! And one of the cook's friends said: 'I'll just have a tiny nibble – such a huge cake – no one'll notice.' And off he went.

And another one of the cook's friends came up to the cake and had a nibble: 'No one'll notice – such a huge cake.' And off he went.

The next morning was the King's birthday, and everyone brought their surprise. The musicians sang a song with no words – which didn't surprise the king at all. The gardener brought in a bunch of blue daffodils which didn't surprise the King much, either. But then the cook came in and said:

'I announce the biggest cake in the world,' and a whole team of horses pulled in the huge cake-box.

But the King just sat there. 'Mmm,' he said. 'Mmmmmmmmmmmmmmmm.'

'Aren't you – I mean don't you – er – wouldn't

you like to have a look, Your Majesty?' said the cook.

'Must I?' said the King, and he slowly got up and came over to the huge box.

'Open the box, then,' said the King.

'Open the box,' said the cook, and four men stepped forward and opened the enormous box.

Where had the cake gone?

And the cook was just about to say it was all a mistake and that he was very sorry, when the King burst out laughing.

'Very good, very good, a trick!' said the King. 'I like it!'

He jumped into the huge box and a moment later came out with something in his hand. Two crumbs and half a currant! 'Very good, very good – the smallest cake in the world in the biggest box. That's what I call a surprise. Well done, cook! Small cake. Big surprise!' But the cook just stood there amazed. What *had* happened to his cake?

The Vain Crocodile

MARGARET MACRAE

There was once a crocodile who lived beside a river in Africa. He was a large crocodile, and he was rather lazy, and very vain. All he ever wanted to do was to lie on the muddy bank in the sunshine, and look at his reflection in the smooth water of the river.

'How handsome I am!' he would say to himself. 'I have the longest tail and strongest teeth in all Africa!'

Now, on the banks of the river there were two villages; one on one side, and one on the other. And every now and then, villagers from one side would want to cross over to the other side to see their friends, or to buy things in the market. They would get into their canoes and paddle across. But as they dipped their paddles into the water – *splish*, *splash*, *splosh*! – the smooth water of the river broke into little waves, which went rippling right up against the bank where the vain crocodile was admiring his reflection in the water.

'My face is going wibbly!' said the crocodile. 'And my tail is wobbly! I don't look handsome any more!'

He was very cross. So he slithered and slid down the muddy bank into the middle of the river. Then, with a swish of his great long tail, he turned the canoe right over, and tipped the villagers into the green water. They all had to swim to the bank, and when they got out they were wet through.

They went to see their king and told him all about it. But the King thought it was very funny. He laughed and laughed when they told him that every time they crossed the river their boats were turned over, and that they got wet through.

'What's wrong with having a swim now and then?' he asked, as he laughed.

But one day, the King had to go across the river to spend the day with his brother on the other side.

He got into the royal canoe, which had been specially decorated for the occasion, and round him sat all his courtiers and his Prime Minister.

They were halfway over when the waves made by their paddles rippled across to where the vain crocodile lay, admiring his reflection in the water. *Wibble-wobble* went the reflection, and the crocodile was very cross.

He slithered and slid down the muddy bank into the green water, and with a swish of his great long tail, he turned the royal canoe right over. The King and all his courtiers fell into the water, and swam for dear life.

When the King got out, he was dripping wet. All his clothes had shrunk, and his crown had dropped off and fallen to the bottom of the river.

'Attishoo!' sneezed the King. He turned to his Prime Minister and said: 'Get rid of that crocodile by tomorrow morning, or you will lose your job!'

The Prime Minister nearly said: 'What's wrong with having a swim now and then?' but he thought perhaps the King wouldn't find it very funny. Instead he went off, dripping with water, to go and speak to the crocodile.

The vain crocodile was happily admiring his

reflection in the river water, which was smooth once more.

The Prime Minister stood in the bushes – not too near, for it isn't a good idea to stand too near a crocodile – and watched him thoughtfully. He looked at the crocodile smiling at his face in the water, then turning round to get the best view of himself, and he had an idea.

The next morning, when it was time for the King to cross the river again to go home, he sent for his Prime Minister.

'Well,' he said, 'have you got rid of that crocodile?'

'I haven't exactly got rid of him, Your Majesty,' said the Prime Minister. 'But I think it will be safe to cross now.'

'It had better be,' said the King grimly.

So off they set in the canoe, and when they reached the middle of the river, they all turned and looked for the crocodile.

There he was, still on the bank – but he wasn't looking in the river at all. He was looking in a huge mirror, propped up against the trees, where his reflection was clearer than ever before. The Prime Minister had put up the mirror while the crocodile was asleep.

The crocodile didn't even turn round to look at the canoe, and the King crossed safely to the other side.

From then on, the crocodile was happy looking at himself in the mirror, and the villagers were happy crossing the river without getting wet.

The Lazy Hippos

SANDRA FERGUSON

Once upon a time there were two lazy hippo-
potamuses: one black hippo who was called
Humphrey, and one white hippo called Henry.
They were so lazy that they used to spend most of
the day just lying in the water-hole. There they lay,
while the rest of their friends worked among the
trees collecting the food and nursing the baby
hippos.

One day two birds flew over the water-hole.
They were looking for somewhere to build their
nests.

'Look at those two islands down in the water-
hole,' said one bird.

'What an excellent place for our nests,' said the
other. 'Nobody could reach them there.'

So they flew down and began to collect twigs and mud with which they built their nests on the two islands.

They didn't know that these islands were the heads of Humphrey and Henry, who were lying in the water-hole fast asleep!

When the nests were finished, the birds each laid an egg. That evening when the hippos wakened, they decided to go for something to eat. Suddenly Humphrey began to chuckle, and then he roared with laughter.

'What are you laughing at?' asked Henry.

'You've grown a hat on your head,' said Humphrey; 'a sort of Scotsman's bonnet.'

Henry said, 'Then you should see your own head. You're wearing a bonnet too!'

And the two friends laughed together. They were

rather proud of their new hats, and especially the lovely shiny blue eggs which nested on the top.

But one night two little birds popped out of the eggs and very soon they began to sing happily and very loudly – so loudly that Henry and Humphrey wakened up.

'Look,' said Henry, 'all our friends are still asleep!'

When at last the sun rose in the sky, Henry and Humphrey had already had their breakfast. Never again did Henry and Humphrey lie asleep while their friends went off to work. The birds who lived in their hats made sure of that!

Grunty Anna

ANDREW DAVIES

This is about a girl called Anna. She's only one.
She's got fat arms and fat legs. Anna doesn't talk
at all. She just grunts. GRUMPH. GRUMPH.

Now Anna has a brother called William. William
is four and a half and he can talk very well. He
knows so many words that he can say almost anything, such as RADIATOR or MERCEDES

BENZ or even HICKETY PICKETY I
SOLICKITY HUMERERJIG.

But Anna just says GRUMPH.

Every day William would say, 'What's your
name, grunty Anna?'

And Anna would just say GRUMPH.

And then he'd say, 'What would you like for
breakfast, grunty Anna?'

And Anna would just say GRUMPH. And
William would laugh his head off, because he
thought that was very funny.

Now one day, not long ago, the whole family,
Anna and William and their mother and father,
were taking a long walk through some fields.

Their mother said, 'Isn't it a lovely day?'

Their father said, 'Weather's holding up well.'

William said, 'I can see a combine harvester.'

And Anna just said GRUMPH.

Then, all of a sudden, they heard shouting
– there were a lot of people running towards
them and the people were shouting, 'Quick,
quick, run, run! The big fierce pig has broken
out. Everybody run!'

But before they could do anything at all, they
saw the pig coming straight towards them. He was

very big – as big as a car. And he did look very fierce. He looked as fierce as a lion.

William said, 'Help, help, the big pig's coming.'

And his mother said, 'Victor, Victor, do something!'

And his father said, 'Look here, er, pig, just you move along there.' But the pig took no notice at all of this.

He came nearer and nearer and *nearer* until he came right up to Anna and stopped.

Anna said GRUMPH.

And the pig said GRUMPH.

And Anna said GRUMPH GRUMPH.

And the pig said GRUMPH GRUMPH.

121

And do you know what he did then? He lay right down and rolled over on his back and Anna gave him a tickle!

And then the farmer came running up and said, 'I've never seen anything like it in my life. But careful, he's still a fierce pig.'

And Anna's mother said, 'Well I never.'

And Anna's father said, 'Her grumph worked.'

And William was very quiet. Now he never laughs at Anna when she goes GRUMPH.

Old Toby and the Hedgehog

KARL WILLIAMS

There was once an old man called Toby, who was a park-keeper, and he looked after a small park in the middle of a town. He mowed the grass and pruned the trees, and made sure that the park always looked tidy.

There were lots of birds and animals who lived in the park, and Old Toby looked after them all. But his special favourite was a hedgehog. Old Toby called him Horace.

Then one day in autumn, the north wind came

rushing through the park, and blew all the leave[s]
off the trees and onto the grass.

It was one of Old Toby's jobs to sweep up th[e]
leaves. He knew it would take him a long time, an[d]
he had just started when a man rode up on a horse[.]

'Good morning,' said the man. 'I am the ne[w]
Superintendent of the parks in this town, and I a[m]
visiting all the park-keepers. How long have yo[u]
been working in this park?'

'Forty-five years,' said Old Toby, proudly.

'Dear me,' said the Park Superintendent, 'W[e]
don't usually keep park-keepers for as long as that[.]
And this park is in a terrible mess. Look at thos[e]
leaves! I'm afraid if they're not cleared up b[y]
tomorrow morning, you had better retire and let [a]
younger man take your place.'

Well, Old Toby was very unhappy at the though[t]
of leaving his park, so he swept all day withou[t]
stopping until it was dark, and he couldn't swee[p]
any more. But there were still leaves all over th[e]
place; Old Toby had only cleared a small corner.

He went home to his cottage, and sat down b[y]
his fire, feeling very sad. Suddenly he heard a sma[ll]
scuffling noise outside, and he saw Horace peepin[g]
round the door.

Old Toby was so glad to see him that he told him what the Superintendent had said. Horace didn't want his friend to leave the park, and so he thought up a plan.

He scampered as fast as he could into the countryside and called on all his friends. Soon Horace had found dozens and dozens of hedgehogs, and he led them all in a line, back through the town to the park.

When they reached the park, some of the hedgehogs curled up into prickly balls and rolled all over the leaves. Their prickles were so sharp that the leaves stuck to them. Then other hedgehogs picked the leaves off and gathered them into neat piles.

The next morning when Old Toby woke up, he was amazed to find that the park was now as neat as a new pin.

The hedgehogs had cleared up all the leaves and gone back to their homes. When the Park Superintendent arrived, he was even more surprised. 'You *have* worked hard! You must stay here as park-keeper,' he said.

So Old Toby kept his job, and when he saw tiny holes in the leaves, he guessed that they had been picked up by sharp prickles.

'Thank you, Horace,' he said to his friend the hedgehog, and from that day on he gave him an extra saucer of milk every morning.

Gail Robinson and Douglas Hill
Coyote the Trickster 95p

The Trickster is a magical creature, with special powers, who appears in various disguises — coyote, raven, hare and fox. He is foolish enough to get into trouble, but cunning enough to get out of the difficulty.

A unique collection of stories from the rich legends and folk tales of the North American Indians.

Terrance Dicks
The Case of the Blackmail Boys 80p

The third exciting story of the now famous Baker Street Irregulars, who model themselves on the helpers of Sherlock Holmes. Organized crime hits the streets and Dan and his friends find themselves on the trail of a master criminal whose methods of extortion and blackmail they are determined to crack. Once again it's a dangerous race as they pit their wits against the professionals.

chosen by Christopher Logue
The Children's Book of Comic Verse 95p

Nothing to do? Nothing to do?
Put some mustard in your shoe,
Fill your pockets full of soot,
Drive a nail into your foot,
Put some sugar in your hair,
And your toys upon the stair . . .

— or laugh, scream and be ill with this super collection of the best comic verse.

Robert Kimmel Smith
Chocolate Fever 80p

The unbelievable happened ! Henry, who loves chocolate in every shape or form, was covered with large, juicy, brown lumps ! A chocolate-eater at breakfast, lunch, tea and supper, now Henry's made medical history : Henry Green, chocolate addict, the first case of 'chocolate fever'. But his problems don't end there – there's a very unusual hijacking . . .

Ann Lawrence
Oggy at Home 70p

Oggy the hedgehog has come a long, long way since the days when he thought Hampstead Heath was the whole world . . . When Oggy is woken up from his long winter sleep, having moved to the countryside, a silly kitten tells him she's 'only exploring' his new home – and Oggy is not very pleased : a well-travelled hedgehog deserves more respect, he thinks, and he sets about teaching Tiggy the scatter-brained kitten a thing or two about the wide, wide world.